First published in Belgium and Holland by Clavis Uitgeverij, Hasselt – Amsterdam, 2017
Copyright © 2017, Clavis Uitgeverij

English translation from the Dutch by Clavis Publishing Inc. New York
Copyright © 2018 for the English language edition: Clavis Publishing Inc. New York

Visit us on the web at www.clavisbooks.com

Sammy in the Spring written and illustrated by Anita Bijsterbosch
Original title: *Sammie in de lente*
Translated from the Dutch by Clavis Publishing

ISBN 978-1-60537-367-6

This book was printed in September 2017 at Wai Man Book Binding (China) Ltd. Flat A, 9/F, Phase 1,
Kwun Tong Industrial Centre, 472-484 Kwun Tong Road, Kwun Tong, Kowloon, H.K.

First Edition
10 9 8 7 6 5 4 3 2 1

SAMMY

in the Spring

Anita Bijsterbosch

Clavis
NEW YORK

Today it's nice and warm outside. Sammy can hear the birds singing. "Hello, little birds, how beautifully you sing!" Sammy says.

"Will you come with me, Hob?"
Sammy asks.
"Let's go play outside."
He puts on his socks and shoes.

Sammy likes riding on his bicycle.
The flowers smell so good!
He can see yellow,
white and pink flowers.

Sammy also likes riding his scooter.
And the butterflies like Sammy.

Sammy and Hob are hiding
behind a bush. Suddenly, Sammy sees
a family of sleeping hedgehogs.
"Hey, hedgehogs, wake up!
Spring has come," Sammy whispers.

Ah, the hedgehogs are awake!
Sammy runs along,
pulling his car behind him.
Hob is having fun
with the hedgehogs.

That's a nice tractor!
Sammy and Hob go for a ride.
Hob is sitting in the back.

Sammy sees some newborn lambs.
How sweet they are!
"Baaa, baaa," the little lambs bleat.
The baby birds are chirping
in their nests.

In the spring, there is always
a lot to do. Sammy likes working
in the garden. He is planting
seedlings in the ground.

Sammy waters the plants
with his watering can
to help them grow.

Sammy and Hob are back inside.
"Come on, Hob, let's wash
our hands and then we
can have dinner," Sammy says.

A nice spring day like today
makes Sammy hungry.
He eats tomatoes, cucumber
and bread. Hob gets an apple.
Have a nice meal, Sammy and Hob!